A Cat About Town

Léa Decan

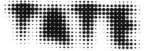

Well, hello! I'm Cat.
And this is Lisa. She takes care of me.
I am HER cat.

But like any busy cat about town . . .

I have quite a lot to do!

In the mornings, I clean my whiskers
and wait by the door.
Lisa usually knows when I want to go out.
She always asks,
"Where are you off to this time, Cat?"

If only she knew!
But I have no time to explain,

I'm such a busy cat.
And I have very important appointments to attend.

On Monday

I visit Sebastian on the fourth floor.
He wears big, square glasses, always carries a book,
and his desk is covered in papers.
He is a writer.

We are both very intellectual . . .

And we understand each other entirely.

On Tuesday

I like to take a stroll downstairs to Mina's balcony.
She has an orange tree, daisies, tulips and lilacs.
On warm spring mornings it smells just wonderful.
It really is the best balcony in town.

Mina gives lots of attention to her flowers . . .

But I like it best when she pays attention to me!

On Wednesday

I go to Granny Yvonne's when the clock strikes noon.
Her granddaughter Lucile comes for lunch,
and they leave the door open just for me.
We feast on roast beef and a crisp green salad,
then have cream cakes for pudding.

I have to say . . .

One always eats very well at Granny Yvonne's!

On Thursday

I enjoy a spot of culture, and slip over to Maud's place.
Her big, colourful studio is a bit of a mess.
She never puts away her brushes and canvases,
but Maud is a talented artist.

Between you and me,
you know I don't like to boast . . .

She's actually VERY famous.
And I'm her favourite subject.

On Friday

The talented musicians of the local string quartet
perform a private concert just for me.
They call it a "rehearsal", and sometimes I join in!
I can never say no to a little Vivaldi or Rossini.

They always reserve me a front row seat.

And a violin case is better than the royal box!

On Saturday

Amélie's boyfriend comes to pick her up for a date,
and I like to visit my dear friend Capucine.
She's the most elegant calico cat with perfect emerald eyes . . .
But, honestly, she's just a friend!

We stroll through the city streets.

Capucine can always make heads turn!

And what about Sunday?

On Sunday, I go home! Because after all, I'm Lisa's cat.

Just Lisa's, and she takes care of me.

To Yvonne

First published 2021 by order of the Tate Trustees
by Tate Publishing, a division of Tate Enterprises Ltd,
Millbank, London SW1P 4RG www.tate.org.uk/publishing

Original text and illustrations copyright
© 2020 Éditions L'Agrume, Sejer
Translation copyright © 2020 Gilberte Bourget

This edition was published by arrangement with
The Picture Book Agency, France.

A catalogue record for this book is available from the British Library

ISBN 978 1 84976 759 0

Distributed in the United States and Canada by ABRAMS, New York
Library of Congress Control Number applied for

Printed and bound in China by C&C Offset Printing Co., Ltd